Dear Parent:

Congratulations! Your child is taking the first steps on an exciting journey. The destination? Independent reading!

STEP INTO READING® will help your child get there. The program offers five steps to reading success. Each step includes fun stories and colorful art. There are also Step into Reading Sticker Books, Step into Reading Math Readers, Step into Reading Write-In Readers, Step into Reading Phonics Readers, and Step into Reading Phonics First Steps! Boxed Sets—a complete literacy program with something for every child.

Learning to Read, Step by Step!

Ready to Read   Preschool–Kindergarten
• big type and easy words • rhyme and rhythm • picture clues
For children who know the alphabet and are eager to begin reading.

Reading with Help   Preschool–Grade 1
• basic vocabulary • short sentences • simple stories
For children who recognize familiar words and sound out new words with help.

Reading on Your Own   Grades 1–3
• engaging characters • easy-to-follow plots • popular topics
For children who are ready to read on their own.

Reading Paragraphs   Grades 2–3
• challenging vocabulary • short paragraphs • exciting stories
For newly independent readers who read simple sentences with confidence.

Ready for Chapters   Grades 2–4
• chapters • longer paragraphs • full-color art
For children who want to take the plunge into chapter books but still like colorful pictures.

STEP INTO READING® is designed to give every child a successful reading experience. The grade levels are only guides. Children can progress through the steps at their own speed, developing confidence in their reading, no matter what their grade.

Remember, a lifetime love of reading starts with a single step!

Special thanks to Vicki Jaeger, Monica Okazaki, Rob Hudnut, Shelley Dvi-Vardhana, Jesyca C. Durchin, Jennifer Twiner McCarron, Shea Wageman, Sharan Wood, Trevor Wyatt, Greg Richardson, Sean Newton, Kelsey Ayukawa, Luke DeWinter, Richard Dixon, Michael Douglas, Scott Eade, Derek Goodfellow, Shaun Martens, Chris McNish, Sarah Miyashita, Pam Prostarr, Craig Shiells, Sheila Turner, Lan Yao, and Walter P. Martishius

www.stepintoreading.com
www.barbie.com

Educators and librarians, for a variety of teaching tools, visit us at
www.randomhouse.com/teachers

Library of Congress Cataloging-in-Publication Data
Alberto, Daisy.
Barbie as the island princess / adapted by Daisy Alberto ; based on the original screenplay by Cliff Ruby & Elana Lesser. — 1st ed.
    p. cm. — (Step into reading. Step 2)
ISBN 978-0-375-84353-2 (trade) — ISBN 978-0-375-94353-9 (lib. bdg.)
I. Ruby, Cliff. II. Lesser, Elana. III. Title. PZ7.A3217Bar 2007 2006036634

Printed in the United States of America

10 9 8 7 6 5 4

First Edition

Barbie as™ The Island Princess

Adapted by Daisy Alberto

Based on the original screenplay
by Cliff Ruby & Elana Lesser

Random House 🏠 New York

After a shipwreck,
a young girl
ended up on an island.

A red panda
and a peacock
watched her.
Their names were
Sagi and Azul.

The girl did not
remember her name.
But a trunk had also
washed up on the sand.

It said "Ro."

So Azul and Sagi
called her Ro.

Years went by.

Ro loved the island.

She played
with Azul, Sagi,
and a baby elephant
named Tika.
She swam.
She climbed trees.
She ate yummy fruit.

Then one day,
another ship
sailed into the cove.

It was Prince Antonio.

He wanted to explore!

11

He walked
through the jungle.
Suddenly he tripped.
Swish!

He slipped and slid
down a bluff.

"Whoa!" he cried.

"Crocodiles!"

Ro saved him.

Ro and the prince
became friends.

He met Azul, Sagi,
and Tika.

The prince invited
them to his kingdom.
Ro was excited.
She wanted to see
the rest of the world.
They sailed away.

Prince Antonio's parents
had a surprise.

They had planned
a wedding
for the prince!

But the prince loved Ro.
She loved him too.

"No," said his father.
"You must marry
a princess."

Ro was heartbroken.

She was not a princess.

And she did not fit in.

The prince was engaged
to Princess Luciana.
Ro liked Luciana.
Ro wished she fit in
like her!

There was a royal ball.
Prince Antonio
danced with Ro.
Luciana's mother saw.
She knew
they were in love.

Luciana's mother
had a plan!
She made all the
animals in the kingdom
fall fast asleep.
Then she blamed Ro.
The king sent Ro away.

Ro and her friends were forced to sail home. They escaped. Dolphins carried them back to the kingdom.

It was the day of the
prince's wedding.
Ro saved the animals.
She told everyone
the truth!

The king was sorry
for what he had done.
Ro forgave him.
And she had a surprise.
She had remembered
her name.
"Please call me Rosella."

One of the guests
was Queen Marissa.
"My daughter's name
was Rosella," she said.
"She was lost at sea."
"Mother!" Ro cried.
Ro had found her family!
She was a princess
after all!

Princess Ro
and Prince Antonio
got married.
They lived
happily ever after.